Brenda's Private Swing

by Bernice Chardiet and Grace Maccarone
pictures by G. Brian Karas

SCHOLASTIC INC.

New York   Toronto   London   Auckland   Sydney

To Jean and Phoebe
B.C. and G.M.

To Adam, Laura, and Leslie
G.B.K.

ISBN 0-590-43304-0

Text copyright © 1990 by Grace Maccarone
and
Bernice Chardiet.
Illustrations copyright © 1990 by Chardiet Unlimited, Inc.
All rights reserved. Published by Scholastic Inc.
Produced by Chardiet Unlimited, Inc.

12 11 10 9 8 7 6 5 4 3   1 2 3 4 5 6/9
Printed in the U.S.A.   08
First Scholastic printing, March 1991

A cool breeze tickled Bunny's face.
It tickled her eyes, her nose, and her lips.
Bunny laughed as she pumped back
and forth on Brenda's new swing set.

Bunny wished she could swing all day.
"You have to stop now!" Brenda said.

"That's mean," said Bunny.
"It's my swing and I can do anything
I want," said Brenda.

"Can I go on the slide?"
Bunny said.
Brenda thought for a minute.
"All right," she said.

Bunny went up the ladder
and down the slide.
Her sneakers stuck as she slid.
It was not a good ride.

Bunny didn't want to slide again.

Bunny sat on the lawn.
She looked at Brenda.
She looked at the empty swing.

Just then, Martin walked by.
"Can I go on your swing?"
he asked Brenda.
"All right," Brenda said.
Martin ran to the swing.
He had a big smile on his face.

Martin started to swing back and forth.
"You have to stop now," said Brenda.
"But I just started," said Martin.
"It's my swing," Brenda said.
"And I want Bunny on it now."

Martin got off the swing.
He went down the slide.
Then he walked up the slide.
"Don't go up the slide that way,"
Brenda said.

Martin sat on top of the slide and
watched the girls swing.
Then he remembered what he had
in his pocket.
A box of Fruity Chewies.
Martin popped a cherry chewie
in his mouth.

Brenda was watching.
"Give me the rest and you can get on
the swing," she said.
Martin quickly slid down.
He gave Brenda the box of chewies.
Bunny had to get off the swing.
She watched until it was time
to go home.

Two days later, Bunny was back at
Brenda's house.
Bunny was having a good long swing.
Then Martin came.
"Can I swing?" he asked.
"Maybe," said Brenda.
Martin took out a box of Gummy Bears.
"You can have these," he said.
"Okay," said Brenda.

This time Bunny was ready.
"I'll give you a chocolate bar," she said.
Brenda took the Gummy Bears.
Then she took the chocolate bar.
"The two of you have to share the
swing," she said.
"It's Martin's turn, now."

Bunny got off the swing.
Martin got on the swing.
Martin swung for a short time.
"Now it's Bunny's turn," Brenda said.

Martin got off the swing.
Bunny got on the swing.
Bunny swung for a short time.
"Now it's Martin's turn," Brenda said.

Then it was Bunny's turn again.
And then it was Martin's turn again.
This isn't much fun at all,
Bunny thought.

Sammy came by and saw them.
He asked to go on the swing.
"Only if you give me candy," Brenda said.
"It's a new rule."

Sammy ran home.
He came back with a bag of jelly beans.
He gave the jelly beans to Brenda.
"May I swing now?" he asked.
"No," said Brenda.
"I hate jelly beans."

Sammy ran home again.
He came back with a Tootsie Roll.
Brenda let him swing.

After that day, everyone who went on Brenda's swing had to give her candy. But one day, Bunny had no candy.

She looked all over the kitchen for something else.
Then she saw the fancy pastries.
Her mother was saving them for company.
But Bunny needed something for Brenda.
She took one pastry.
It had layers of cream and flaky crust.
The top had white frosting with chocolate squiggles.
It was Bunny's favorite.

Brenda liked the pastry very much.
Bunny was swinging back and forth
when Martin came by.

"What do you have for me?"
Brenda asked.
"My mother wouldn't let me have any
candy today," Martin said.
"Too bad," said Brenda.
"Then you can't swing."
"*Please*," said Martin.
"I'll give you something tomorrow.
Please!"
"No," said Brenda.

Bunny was having a long swing.
But this time it wasn't fun.
She felt bad because Martin looked so sad.
And she felt bad because she had taken
the pastry.

That night, Bunny told her mother,
"I took a pastry."
"That's all right," her mother said.
"I bought an extra one just for you.
But next time, you should tell me first."

The next day, Bunny and Martin were
having lunch at school.
"What do you have for Brenda today?"
Bunny asked.
Martin looked in his lunch box.
"A box of Fruity Chewies," he said.

"I have two chocolate marshmallow cookies," said Bunny.

"But I wish I could keep them for myself."

"Me, too," said Martin.

Just then, Brenda came by.
"Oooh! My favorites," she said.

Brenda reached for the Fruity Chewies.
"No," said Martin.
Brenda reached for a cookie.
"No," said Bunny.
"You'll be sorry when you want to use my swing," Brenda said.

"No, we won't!" Bunny shouted.

Brenda stuck out her tongue and
walked away.

"Let's play checkers after school,"
Martin said.
"Okay," said Bunny. "Would you like a
chocolate marshmallow cookie, Martin?"
"Yes," said Martin. "Have a Fruity Chewie.
Bossy Brenda can play by herself, today."